HUMAN OR MACHINE TRAP

AKHIL SAJAN

JAGDISH SHETTY

Contents

Foreword

The world is changing faster than we can often comprehend. Technology has become an inseparable part of our lives, shaping our identities, relationships, and the very future we imagine for ourselves. As we wrote Human or Machine Trap, we found ourselves reflecting on these changes the promises of technology, as well as the hidden risks that come with it.

Set in the bustling, ever-transforming city of Mumbai, Human or Machine Trap began as a simple "what if." What if technology could cross boundaries we never imagined? What if it starts to control not only our actions but our choices, our very humanity? This story is not just a journey of one character but a dive into the delicate dance between human nature and machine innovation.

Creating this novel was both a challenge and a joy. The characters became friends, their dilemmas my own, and every twist in the plot felt like a new discovery. I hope this story raises questions that resonate with you, sparking curiosity about the world we are building.

Thank you for embarking on this journey with me, for stepping into a world where humanity and technology stand on a knife's edge. Human or Machine Trap is more than a story—it's an invitation to explore what lies beyond the obvious, to question, and to wonder.

Enjoy the story, and thank you for reading.

Akhil Sajan , Jagdish Shetty

Preface

As our world grows increasingly interconnected and technology becomes a permanent extension of our daily lives, the line between human and machine continues to blur. We live in an age of rapid technological advancement, where the allure of efficiency and progress often overshadows the importance of our humanity. This book, Human or Machine Trap, delves into this shifting landscape and asks the question: What happens when technology becomes more than a tool and starts defining who we are?

Set against the dynamic backdrop of Mumbai, a city where tradition and innovation collide, this story follows a young woman, Ava, as she navigates a hidden world of secrets, loyalty, and power. Ava's journey is a reflection of the struggle many of us face in preserving our individuality and agency in a world increasingly driven by machines. The characters in this novel each face their own versions of this challenge, questioning who they are and who they're becoming under the influence of unseen forces.

Human or Machine Trap is not just a tale of technology but of human resilience and the choices we make to protect what defines us. As you turn these pages, we invite you to ponder where you stand in this evolving world and to ask yourself what it truly means to be human.

Acknowledgements

Creating Human or Machine Trap has been a journey of discovery, growth, and perseverance, and we are deeply grateful to everyone who helped make this book a reality.
To our family and friends, for their unwavering support and encouragement. Your faith in us has been a constant source of motivation.
I would like to express my deepest gratitude to **Shippu Bushan** for her invaluable guidance, insightful feedback, and meticulous editing throughout the creation of this book.
And to my readers, who give life to these pages with your imagination and curiosity—this book is for you
With gratitude,
Akhil Sajan, Jagdish Shetty

Prologue

The vibrant streets of Mumbai pulsed with life—a kaleidoscope of colors, sounds, and stories woven into the fabric of the city. Street vendors lined the bustling sidewalks, hawking everything from spices to trinkets. Motorbikes zipped through the crowded alleys, and the distant honking of rickshaws formed a chaotic symphony. Amid this animated beauty, however, a darker reality thrived, hidden beneath the city's glittering facade.

In Mumbai's shadowed corners, secrets were traded like currency. Deals were made in whispers, fortunes decided behind closed doors, and lives manipulated with precision. This was the hidden underworld, where the powerful used advanced technology not to serve humanity but to control it. For those who fell victim to it, hope was often a fading memory, lost in the relentless pace of survival.

Ava was seventeen and an orphan, living in this world without truly understanding its depths. The orphanage was her only constant, a sanctuary from the struggles of daily life. With her best friend Alex by her side, she faced Mumbai's highs and lows, their bond forged in trust and mutual dreams. To her, the city was both a home and a maze, each corner holding a new mystery, a new story.

But on one fateful evening, everything changed.

Alex's warm, easygoing smile hid a secret Ava never suspected. His loyalty masked something darker—something that would unravel the simplicity of her world. As the sun dipped below the Arabian Sea, casting a golden glow over the skyline, Ava's fate was sealed. She stood on the edge of an abyss she didn't even know existed, unaware of the shadow that had been following her.

And in that moment, the first threads of her carefully woven life began to unravel, setting off a chain of events that would force her to confront her deepest fears. The underbelly of Mumbai wasn't just a hidden layer of the city—it was a machine, one that could swallow the unsuspecting whole.

As darkness fell, Ava's journey into the unknown had begun.

ONE

THE SECRET WITHIN MUMBAI

The streets of Mumbai were a living, breathing tapestry of color and sound, a city that pulsed like a heartbeat, its rhythm never faltering. The evening lights cast a warm glow overcrowded alleys, and vendors called out, their voices rising above the hum of engines and laughter. This was Ava's world, her familiar chaos, her home.

For 17-year-old Ava, life was uncomplicated, if a little confined. She lived in the Mahatma Orphanage, a modest building with peeling paint and creaky floors that stood like a silent witness to the years gone by. Ava had learned to adapt to its rhythms—the early morning chores, the bustling mornings at school, and the comforting quiet of nights spent in the dormitory. Her days were punctuated by the small joys of friendship, laughter, and dreams of a future that felt just out of reach.

But today, something tugged at her, a feeling she couldn't quite shake. Maybe it was the way Alex had avoided her at lunch, his eyes darting away whenever she caught his gaze. Or maybe it was the strange heaviness in his voice when they spoken that morning, a shadow of something hidden. Alex was her best friend, the only family she'd known since they were small children. They'd shared countless stories, secrets, and dreams under the sprawling banyan tree in the orphanage yard, the only constant in their ever-shifting world. But recently, Alex had become a mystery to her, slipping away like sand between her fingers.

That evening, Ava found herself wandering through the narrow lanes outside the orphanage, hoping the familiar chaos would drown out her unease. The night market was in full swing, and the air was rich with the smell of spicy chaat and fresh naan sizzling over hot griddles. But even amidst the bustling crowds, Ava couldn't escape her thoughts.

As she rounded a corner, a flicker of movement caught her eye. It was Alex, standing under a flickering streetlight, speaking to a figure cloaked in shadow. The sight stopped her in her tracks. Alex was always cautious, and he had always kept to himself around strangers. This scene felt wrong, somehow. She couldn't quite hear their conversation, but the urgency in Alex's tone and the subtle tension in his stance made her pulse quicken.

"Alex?" she called out softly, stepping forward. But before her voice could carry, the stranger turned and disappeared into the alleyway, vanishing as quickly as he had appeared.

Alex's head snapped toward her, his eyes widening. For a split second, his expression was one of shock—almost fear—but then he quickly masked it with a smile that didn't reach his eyes. "Ava! What are you doing here?" he asked, too casually, as if trying to pretend everything was normal.

Ava frowned, crossing her arms. "I could ask you the same question. Who was that?"

Alex shifted uncomfortably, rubbing the back of his neck. "Oh, just... someone from school. Nothing important."

"Really?" Ava's tone was skeptical. "I've never seen you talk to anyone like that before. What's going on?"

He hesitated, glancing over his shoulder as if expecting someone to be listening. "It's nothing, Ava. Seriously. Don't worry about it."

But Ava's instincts told her otherwise. She could feel the walls he was putting up between them, walls that hadn't been there before. Frustrated, she pressed on, hoping to breach his defenses. "Come on, Alex. It's me. You know you can tell me anything."

For a moment, he softened, the mask slipping as he looked at her with the vulnerability she recognized. But just as quickly, his expression hardened, a guarded look taking over. "I'll explain someday, Ava. Just... trust me, okay?"

With that, he turned and walked away, leaving her standing alone under the streetlight, the hum of the city filling the silence he left behind. Ava watched him go, confusion swirling in her mind, a sense of dread settling in her chest.

Back at the orphanage, sleep evaded Ava, her mind replaying the evening's events. She lay on her narrow cot, staring at the cracked ceiling, questions swirling in her head. She wanted to believe Alex's assurances, but the uncertainty gnawed at her. What was he hiding? And why did it feel like he was slipping away, caught in something bigger than either of them?

As the night deepened, Ava's thoughts shifted, drifting toward a memory. She remembered one of the nights she and Alex had stayed up late, talking about their dreams. They had promised to stay together, to be there for each other no matter what. It was a promise that felt unbreakable—until tonight.

And so, with a heavy heart and an uneasy mind, Ava finally drifted off, unaware that this moment marked the end of one chapter in her life and the beginning of a journey that would unravel every truth she thought she knew. A journey where secrets would come to light, bonds would be tested, and the line between human and machine would blur in ways she could never have imagined.

TWO

A HIDDEN TRUTH

The next day, Ava tried to push the previous evening's encounter from her mind. But the image of Alex's guarded expression lingered, like a shadow she couldn't shake. School felt different—every laugh, every exchange of gossip among her classmates, felt trivial against the weight of her worries. She found herself glancing around, half-expecting to see Alex speaking to that stranger again, but he seemed to have retreated into his own world.

Ava made her way through the crowded hallways of St. Joseph's High School, the sounds of lockers slamming and voices rising fading into a distant buzz. She spotted Alex at their usual lunch table, but today he sat with his back turned, his attention focused on something—or someone—across the cafeteria. A knot tightened in her stomach. Had he found new friends already, or was he still involved with that mysterious group?

"Hey, Ava!" chirped Meera, one of her classmates, pulling her from her thoughts. "You're looking a bit lost today. Everything okay?"

Ava forced a smile, masking her unease. "Yeah, just tired, I guess."

As they chatted, her eyes darted back to Alex. He was now engaged in a deep conversation with a boy she didn't recognize, their laughter ringing out like an echo of what she once shared with him. Something twisted in her chest, a mix of jealousy and worry. She had always been able to talk to him about anything, but now it felt like he was slipping away.

"Want to sit with us?" Meera asked, breaking into Ava's thoughts.

"Sure," Ava replied, though her mind was still on Alex. She needed to find a way to talk to him, to understand what was happening.

After school, as the sun dipped low in the sky, painting the horizon in shades of orange and pink, Ava made her way to the library—a quiet sanctuary where she often sought solace. She sat at a table in the corner, pretending to read, but her thoughts were miles away, consumed by worry.

Then, in a moment of determination, she pulled out her phone and texted Alex.

"Can we talk? I need to understand what's going on."

Her heart raced as she hit send, but she was met with silence. Minutes passed, stretching into what felt like hours. Finally, her phone buzzed.

"Busy right now. Let's catch up later?"

Ava's heart sank. "Later" felt like a dismissal, a way to avoid the conversation she desperately needed.

She left the library, frustration boiling inside her. Determined to confront him, she decided to head toward the community center where the orphanage organized after-school activities. It was a popular spot for the kids, and she hoped Alex would be there.

When she arrived, the familiar sounds of laughter and chatter filled the air, mingling with the smell of freshly cooked snacks. She spotted Alex in the corner, surrounded by a small group of boys, but he seemed distant, laughing at jokes she couldn't hear.

With a deep breath, Ava approached, trying to catch his eye. As she stepped closer, she caught snippets of their conversation, words that sent a chill down her spine.

"... you should have seen the look on her face when I showed her the prototype," Alex was saying, his voice animated yet edged with something Ava couldn't quite place.

"Yeah, man! She was totally freaked out," another boy replied, laughter echoing around them.

Ava's heart raced. Prototype? What prototype? She felt her pulse quicken, each beat echoing her growing unease. Gathering her courage, she interrupted, "Alex, can we talk? Please?"

He turned, surprise etched on his face, but it quickly faded to a practiced neutrality. "Uh, can it wait, Ava? We're just hanging out."

"No, it can't," she insisted, frustration spilling over. "I need to know what's going on with you. This isn't just about hanging out anymore."

The laughter died down, and the boys exchanged glances, sensing the tension. Alex sighed, rubbing the back of his neck, a telltale sign of his discomfort. "Fine. Let's step outside."

Ava followed him outside, the noise of the community center fading as they moved into the quiet of the evening. The air was thick with anticipation, and as the sun set, the sky darkened, the stars slowly twinkling to life.

"What's this really about, Ava?" Alex said, his voice low. "I told you it's nothing."

"Nothing?" she echoed incredulously. "You've been acting so strange lately, and I saw you last night. Who was that person? What prototype?"

He hesitated, a flicker of something—fear?—crossing his features. "It's complicated."

"Then make it simple! You can't just shut me out. I thought we were best friends. I thought we promised to be there for each other."

For a moment, silence hung between them, heavy and palpable. Alex looked away, his expression clouded. "Ava, there are things happening that you don't understand. I... I can't explain everything right now. Just trust me."

"Trust you?" she exclaimed, her voice rising. "Trust you to what? Get involved in something dangerous? You're not the Alex I know. This isn't just about you anymore!"

His gaze snapped back to hers, and in that moment, she saw something raw, something desperate in his eyes. "Ava, please! I'm trying to protect you."

"Protect me? From what? From you?"

Before he could respond, a loud shout erupted from the community center. The boys were calling for Alex, and he glanced over his shoulder, the moment lost. "I have to go. Just... don't worry about me, okay?"

With that, he turned and jogged back inside, leaving Ava standing alone in the growing darkness, a mixture of anger and fear coursing through her.

She stared after him, her heart heavy with uncertainty. How had they gone from sharing secrets under the banyan tree to standing worlds apart?

As she walked back to the orphanage, her mind raced with possibilities. There was more to this than Alex was letting on, and she was determined to find out the truth. She had to uncover the secrets hiding in the shadows of their friendship, even if it meant diving into a world that threatened to pull her under.

In the days to come, Ava knew she would have to confront the reality of what was happening in Alex's life—a reality that was darker and more complex than she could have ever imagined.

THREE

A Betrayal Unveiled

In the days that followed her tense conversation with Alex, Ava couldn't shake the feeling that something terrible was unfolding right in front of her. The shadowy figure, the whispered secrets, and the evasive answers—all of it gnawed at her. She knew she needed to get to the bottom of this, even if it meant pushing the boundaries of their friendship.

One evening, as the sun dipped low over Mumbai, casting long shadows across the narrow alleyways, Ava decided it was time to take matters into her own hands. She slipped out of the orphanage, her heart pounding with anticipation and fear. She had noticed Alex's routine over the past few days and knew where he might be tonight—near the abandoned factory on the outskirts of the city.

The factory loomed in the distance as she approached, its once-thriving walls now crumbling and covered in graffiti. The place had been abandoned for years, but tonight, faint lights flickered from within. Ava crept closer, her footsteps muffled by the layer of dust and debris on the ground.

Peering through a broken window, she saw Alex standing among a small group of people. Her breath hitched as she realized that he wasn't alone. There were men and women dressed in sleek, dark clothing, holding what looked like high-tech devices, their faces illuminated by the cold blue glow of screens. The leader of the group, a tall man with a calculating expression, handed Alex a small metallic device—something that looked like a microchip but with intricate wiring and a faint pulsing light.

"This," the man said in a low voice, "is the first step toward true power. With this prototype, you'll be able to connect directly with *The Machina's* network."

Ava's stomach twisted. *The Machina.* She had heard whispers of them in the streets—a secretive organization rumored to experiment with advanced technology, blending human minds with machine intelligence. People spoke of them in hushed tones, calling them the "shadow rulers" of the city, pulling strings from behind the scenes.

She watched as Alex took the microchip, his face unreadable. He turned it over in his hands, examining it with a strange mixture of fascination and reluctance. "Are you sure this will... work?" he asked, his voice a shaky whisper.

The leader's gaze hardened. "We don't have time for doubts, Alex. You wanted to be part of something bigger, didn't you? This is your chance. Once you're connected, there's no going back."

Ava's heart sank as she realized the depth of Alex's involvement. He wasn't just dabbling in something risky; he was diving headfirst into a world that could consume him. Her hands clenched into fists, anger and betrayal boiling within her. She wanted to barge in, to shake him, to demand that he explain himself. But she knew she couldn't. Not yet.

The leader continued, his tone smooth and persuasive. "With this connection, you'll be more than just a bystander. You'll have access to information, to influence. You'll be part of the future."

Alex nodded, his expression steeling as he placed the microchip in his pocket. "I understand. I'm ready."

Ava backed away from the window, her heart hammering in her chest. She felt as if she were falling, the ground slipping out from under her. She had always trusted Alex, had always believed in him, and yet here he was, willing to give up his humanity for a promise of power.

She turned and hurried back down the alley, her mind racing. The world around her felt different now, darker and colder. She realized that Alex's actions weren't just dangerous for him—they threatened everyone around him, including her.

Back at the orphanage, she lay awake, staring at the cracked ceiling, her mind replaying the scene at the factory. She knew she had to confront Alex, to make him understand the dangers of *The Machina*. But she also realized something chilling: Alex might not want to be saved.

FOUR

INTO THE LION'S DEN

Ava spent the following days in a daze, unable to shake the image of Alex and that strange group from her mind. Every time she closed her eyes, she saw the cold gleam of the microchip and the menacing figure of the leader, his words echoing in her mind: *With this connection, you'll be part of the future.*

At school, Alex remained elusive. He seemed to sense her watching him and avoided her gaze, his face distant and expression closed off. Ava's frustration grew with each passing day. She knew that if she waited any longer, she might lose him completely. She needed answers—and fast.

That evening, she decided to confront him directly. She cornered him in an empty hallway after school, blocking his way as he tried to slip past.

"Alex, we need to talk," she said, her voice barely concealing her anger.

He glanced around, clearly uncomfortable. "Ava, not here. Please, just leave it alone."

"No," she replied, her voice firm. "I saw you at the factory. I saw everything. You're involved with *The Machina*, aren't you?"

His face went pale, and for a moment, he looked like the Alex she knew—the one who used to confide in her, the one who had shared her dreams. But just as quickly, he masked his fear, his eyes narrowing. "You don't understand, Ava. This isn't something you can just waltz into and question."

"Then help me understand!" she pleaded. "This... this isn't you, Alex. What happened to us? What happened to the promises we made to each other?"

He sighed, running a hand through his hair. "Ava, things have changed. This is bigger than you or me. *The Machina...* they're offering a way out, a chance to be something more."

"A chance to be controlled, you mean," she shot back, her voice trembling. "I don't know what they promised you, but this isn't worth losing yourself."

A tense silence hung between them. For a moment, Alex seemed to waver, a flicker of doubt crossing his face. But then his expression hardened, his eyes growing cold. "You wouldn't understand, Ava. You don't know what it's like to feel powerless."

She took a step back, feeling the weight of his words. She had always thought she knew him, understood his fears and insecurities. But this was something different—something darker.

"Fine," she said quietly, her voice laced with hurt. "If you won't help me understand, then I'll find out on my own."

Before he could respond, she turned and walked away, her heart pounding with a mixture of anger and determination. She didn't know how, but she was going to get to the bottom of this. She wasn't going to let *The Machina* take him without a fight.

That Night

Back at the orphanage, Ava paced in her small room, her mind racing. If she was going to uncover *The Machina's* secrets, she needed information. She pulled out her laptop, fingers trembling as she typed *The Machina* into the search bar.

Most of what she found was obscure conspiracy theories and rumors on fringe websites. People spoke of *The Machina* as if it were a ghost—a powerful, invisible force that could manipulate everything from technology to people's minds. Some claimed they had developed advanced AI capable of merging with human consciousness, creating a hybrid that was neither fully human nor machine.

Ava shuddered, her stomach twisting as she read more. She couldn't believe Alex would be drawn to something so dangerous. And yet, she remembered the look in his eyes—the desperation that had driven him to make this choice.

As she scrolled through the forums, she came across a post that caught her attention. It was written by someone named "Watcher," and it seemed to contain a warning:

"To those who seek The Machina, beware. Their promises come at a cost. They control you from within, leaving you a shell of who you once were. They'll offer power, but it's a trap. They'll make you think it's your choice, but in the end, you're just another cog in their machine."

A chill ran down her spine. Could this be what Alex was walking into? A life where he'd be stripped of his freedom, his individuality, his very humanity? She knew she couldn't let that happen.

Determined, Ava decided to find this "Watcher." If anyone could help her understand the true nature of *The Machina*, it was this person. She sent a message, hoping that they would respond.

Days Later

After days of anxious waiting, she received a reply.

"If you're truly seeking the truth, meet me at the old lighthouse near Worli. Midnight. Come alone."

Ava's heart pounded as she read the message. She knew this was risky, possibly even dangerous, but she didn't care. This was her only lead, her only hope of saving Alex.

That night, she slipped out of the orphanage under the cover of darkness, her footsteps light as she made her way through the sleeping streets of Mumbai. The city was quiet, a stark contrast to the vibrant energy of the day, and the silence felt eerie, like the calm before a storm.

As she approached the old lighthouse, she saw a figure waiting in the shadows. The person wore a hood, their face obscured, but she could see the glint of wary eyes watching her.

"You're the one who sent the message?" she asked, her voice barely a whisper.

The figure nodded, stepping forward. "You're looking for *The Machina*," they said, their voice low and guarded. "But be careful, girl. Once you go down this path, there's no turning back."

Ava squared her shoulders, determination hardening her gaze. "I need to save my friend. He's... he's been taken in by them."

The figure's eyes softened, and for a moment, Ava thought she saw a flicker of understanding. "Then you're braver than most. But bravery alone won't be enough. *The Machina* is not just a group—it's a system. A network that feeds of fear, off the need for control."

Ava swallowed, feeling the weight of his words. "Then tell me what I need to do."

The figure hesitated, as if weighing her determination. Finally, they nodded. "Tomorrow night, *The Machina* will host an initiation ceremony in the very heart of Mumbai's underbelly. They'll bring in new recruits—your friend will likely be there. But getting in won't be easy. You'll need to be prepared for what you'll see."

Ava's heart raced as she took in the instructions. She didn't know what awaited her, but she was ready to face it. She would do whatever it took to save Alex from the shadows of *The Machina*.

FIVE

THE INITIATION

The night air was thick with anticipation as Ava made her way to the heart of Mumbai's underbelly. Following the mysterious figure's instructions, she navigated winding alleys and shadowed pathways until she arrived at an inconspicuous building nestled between two crumbling warehouses. She could hear murmurs inside, a blend of voices that sent chills down her spine.

Disguising herself in a hooded jacket, she slipped through the side entrance and blended in with a small crowd moving down a dimly lit corridor. Her heart thumped as she tried to suppress the rising fear. She was closer than ever to the truth but also stepping into unknown territory, risking her own safety to reach Alex.

The corridor opened into a vast, cavernous room filled with people. A stage stood at the far end, shrouded in shadows, while strange symbols illuminated the walls in an eerie, electric blue. As Ava glanced around, she recognized some of the attendees—not only outcasts and misfits but also individuals who exuded power, dressed in sharp suits and elegant attire. It was as if *The Machina* cast a wide net, attracting people from every corner of society.

Ava's gaze darted through the crowd, searching for Alex. She couldn't see him yet, but she knew he had to be there. Her stomach twisted with unease, but she steeled herself. She couldn't afford to panic now.

The crowd fell silent as a figure stepped onto the stage. Ava's eyes widened—it was the man from the factory, the one who had given Alex the microchip. His presence was commanding, his voice calm yet filled with a subtle threat.

"Tonight," he began, his voice resonating through the room, "we welcome new recruits into *The Machina*. Each of you has been chosen because you see beyond the limitations of ordinary life. You understand that true power lies in knowledge, in control. And through us, you can have it all."

A hush fell over the room, a collective breath held in anticipation. Ava's pulse quickened. She wanted to run, to shout for Alex to leave, but she forced herself to stay silent, to watch and listen.

The man raised his hand, and from the shadows, a group of individuals stepped forward, each carrying a small device. Ava's heart sank as she recognized the microchips—sleek, metallic, with the faint glow she'd seen before. One by one, the recruits were given a chip, their expressions a mixture of fear and exhilaration.

Finally, she spotted Alex near the front, his face illuminated by the soft light of the chip in his hand. He looked both entranced and nervous, his gaze fixed on the device as though it held the answers to every question he had ever asked.

What are you doing, Alex? Ava thought, feeling her heart constrict. She wanted to reach out, to scream his name, but she knew that any wrong move would give her away. Instead, she clenched her fists, willing herself to wait.

The man on stage continued. "This device is more than just technology. It is a doorway—a bridge that will connect your mind to *The Machina's* network. You will be part of something greater than yourself, part of a power that controls the flow of information, the very essence of reality."

Ava felt a chill run down her spine as the recruits, one by one, placed the chips against their temples, their faces flickering with the pale blue glow. Each person's expression shifted, eyes glassy as they connected to the network. Ava watched in horror as they transformed, their movements stiff, robotic, yet filled with an eerie sense of purpose.

She saw Alex hesitating, the chip trembling in his hand. His gaze flickered, and for a moment, she thought he might resist, might reject the allure of this dark power. But the man on stage, sensing Alex's hesitation, locked eyes with him, his voice soothing yet forceful.

"Don't fear it," he urged. "You're meant for this, Alex. You've been searching for a purpose, for a way out. This is it."

Ava's heart pounded as she watched Alex's expression waver. She wanted to scream at him, to shake him out of his trance. She felt the weight of her silence, each second slipping by as Alex's grip on his identity weakened. She knew this was her only chance—she had to act.

Summoning her courage, she pushed through the crowd, her gaze fixed on Alex. She didn't care if anyone saw her now. All that mattered was reaching him, breaking through the fog of deception that held him captive.

"Alex!" she whispered urgently, grabbing his arm just as he raised the chip to his temple.

He jerked back, startled. For a moment, he blinked, the spell breaking as he stared at her in disbelief. "Ava? What are you...?"

"Don't do it," she pleaded, her voice barely audible over the murmurs of the crowd. "This isn't you. You don't need this."

He looked down at the chip in his hand, confusion clouding his gaze. "But they promised... they promised I'd finally be someone, Ava. That I'd have control, power."

"They're lying to you, Alex. Look around." She gestured at the others, their eyes vacant, their movements unnaturally synchronized. "Do you think they're free? They're nothing but puppets now, controlled by *The Machina*."

He swallowed, glancing back at the stage where the leader watched them, his eyes narrowing with suspicion. Alex's grip loosened on the chip, and Ava felt a flicker of hope.

But before he could make a decision, the leader's voice cut through the air, cold and commanding. "Is there a problem here?"

The crowd parted, eyes turning toward them. Ava felt the weight of a hundred stares pressing down on her, but she held her ground, refusing to release Alex's arm.

The leader stepped down from the stage, his gaze icy as he approached. "You must be the friend Alex spoke of," he said, his tone mocking. "The one who thinks she can save him."

Ava's jaw clenched, her eyes blazing with defiance. "I won't let you take him."

The leader chuckled, a chilling sound that echoed through the room. "Take him? My dear, Alex chose this path. He's free to leave—if he wants to." He turned to Alex, his gaze penetrating. "Well, Alex? Do you want to go back to your old life? Or do you want the future we promised?"

Alex's face twisted in torment, caught between the promises of *The Machina* and the plea in Ava's eyes. His hand trembled as he stared at the chip, his mind warring with itself.

Ava squeezed his arm, her voice a fierce whisper. "Alex, listen to me. They're only using you. Whatever they've promised, it's a lie. You don't need them to be strong."

He closed his eyes, taking a shuddering breath. When he opened them again, Ava saw a spark of clarity.

Without a word, he dropped the chip, letting it fall to the ground, where it shattered into a thousand tiny pieces.

The leader's face darkened, a dangerous glint in his eyes. "You'll regret this, both of you."

But Ava didn't care. Grabbing Alex's hand, she pulled him through the crowd, weaving past the stunned recruits and out of the dark, oppressive space. They ran into the night, away from the clutches of *The Machina*, their breaths coming in ragged gasps as they finally tasted freedom.

SIX

THE BURDEN OF FREEDOM

The sky was a dark canvas as Ava and Alex finally slowed down, their breaths heavy and ragged. They'd run through narrow alleys and deserted streets, putting as much distance as possible between themselves and *The Machina's* shadowed lair. They stopped near a secluded park, hidden from view by thick trees. The silence here felt foreign after the chaos they had left behind.

For a moment, they stood in silence, each grappling with their own thoughts. Ava glanced at Alex, whose face was still pale, his expression haunted. He looked as if he was waking from a nightmare he couldn't quite remember, yet the scars of it lingered on his face.

"I... I don't know how to thank you, Ava," he said finally, his voice barely a whisper. "If you hadn't been there..."

Ava shook her head, giving him a reassuring smile. "Don't. You'd have done the same for me."

Alex nodded, though the guilt in his eyes was unmistakable. "I should have listened to you. They had me trapped in this idea that joining them was the only way I could ever... belong somewhere."

"It's not your fault, Alex," Ava said softly. "They know how to prey on people's fears and insecurities. But you're stronger than that."

He looked down, studying his hands as if they held the answers to questions he hadn't dared to ask. "The things they promised—control, a way to be... more—I wanted that so badly. I thought maybe this time, I could be someone who mattered."

"You already matter, Alex," she said, her voice steady. "To me and to everyone who knows the real you."

He looked at her, a faint glimmer of gratitude in his eyes. But before he could respond, they both heard it—the faint crunch of footsteps on gravel, somewhere in the darkness beyond the trees. They froze, exchanging a glance of alarm.

"Do you think they... followed us?" Alex whispered.

Ava's heart raced. The adrenaline that had just begun to subside now surged through her veins again. She scanned the shadows, straining to see any movement. "We can't stay here," she murmured, grabbing his hand. "Let's go."

They slipped through the trees, moving as silently as possible, their senses heightened. The city lights flickered in the distance, a beacon of safety they couldn't quite reach. Every shadow seemed to hold a threat, every sound made their hearts jump.

As they turned a corner, a figure stepped into their path, blocking their way. It was a young man, roughly their age, dressed in casual clothes that didn't quite disguise the sharp alertness in his eyes. Ava tightened her grip on Alex's hand, her body tensing.

"Are you Ava and Alex?" the stranger asked, his voice low.

They exchanged a quick, uncertain glance. Finally, Ava spoke, her voice guarded. "Who wants to know?"

The young man raised his hands in a gesture of peace. "Relax. I'm on your side. My name is Rehan. I was sent by... someone who knows what you're up against."

Alex frowned, stepping forward. "Sent by who?"

Rehan's eyes darted around, as if checking for eavesdroppers. "There's a network of people who have been resisting *The Machina* for years—people who know what they're really capable of. I'm part of that network, and I'm here to help."

Ava's mind reeled. "Why should we trust you?"

Rehan sighed, looking directly into her eyes. "Because you don't have many other options. *The Machina* doesn't take kindly to betrayal, and they're probably already searching for you."

The mention of *The Machina* sent a chill down her spine. The leader's words echoed in her mind: *You'll regret this, both of you.*

"Look," Rehan continued, his voice urgent. "You both barely escaped with your lives tonight. If they find you again, they won't give you another chance."

Ava's grip on Alex's hand tightened as she weighed their options. Rehan's words made sense, but trust was not something she was willing to give easily, especially now. "What exactly do you want from us?"

Rehan looked around once more, as though the trees might have ears. "For now, I just want to get you somewhere safe. There's a place nearby where we can lay low and figure out our next steps. If you want answers, I can help you get them. But staying here will only make you a target."

Alex turned to Ava, his eyes filled with a mixture of fear and hope. "I think... I think we should go with him," he said, his voice barely above a whisper.

Ava hesitated. Every instinct told her to run, to hide, but there was something in Rehan's eyes—a kind of determination, a shared fear—that made her pause. She nodded reluctantly. "Fine. But if this is a trap…"

Rehan shook his head. "You have my word. I'm one of the few people who wants *The Machina* gone as much as you do."

He led them away from the park, through a maze of back alleys and narrow streets, until they reached a small, abandoned building. The place was rundown, with faded walls and cracked windows, but it felt safe, isolated from the rest of the city. Rehan opened a door and motioned for them to enter.

Inside, they found a small room with only a few pieces of furniture—a table, a couch, and a dim light casting soft shadows on the walls. Rehan closed the door, locking it behind them.

"This will be our base for now," he said, turning to face them. "There's food and water here, and it's secure. You'll be safe here until we figure out our next move."

Ava sank onto the couch, her mind racing. The events of the night felt surreal, like a dream she couldn't wake up from. She glanced at Alex, who seemed equally dazed.

Rehan pulled up a chair, sitting across from them. "I know you're both tired, but there's something you need to know."

They looked at him, waiting.

"The chip—the one they tried to implant in you, Alex—it's not just a device. It's part of a system designed to control people's thoughts, their actions, even their emotions. Once it's implanted, they have access to your mind, your memories. You become a part of *The Machina* network, a tool they can use however they want."

Ava felt a surge of anger, the pieces clicking into place. "So they would have made Alex a puppet."

"Exactly," Rehan replied grimly. "*The Machina* isn't just after power—they want to control every aspect of people's lives, to turn society into something they can shape to their will."

Alex shuddered, his face pale. "But... why me? I'm nobody."

Rehan's gaze softened. "*The Machina* preys on people who feel like they don't belong, people who are searching for purpose. It's how they recruit, how they expand their influence."

Ava clenched her fists, fury burning in her chest. "We have to stop them. We can't let them keep doing this to people."

Rehan nodded. "That's why I'm here. We have a small network, people who've managed to evade *The Machina's* control. But it's not easy. They're powerful, and they have eyes everywhere. It'll take more than just courage to bring them down."

Ava met Rehan's gaze, her voice firm. "Then we'll do whatever it takes.

SEVEN

SHADOWS OF THE PAST

Inside the cramped safety of their temporary hideout, Ava, Alex, and Rehan sat in a tense silence. The weight of what they'd just learned from Rehan lingered in the air. Ava could see the turmoil in Alex's eyes—a mixture of anger, confusion, and a hint of something else: fear.

Rehan leaned forward, his face solemn. "If you want to take down *The Machina*, you need to understand how far they're willing to go. They don't care about lives—they care about loyalty and control. And anyone who questions them is erased."

Ava clenched her fists. "We can't let them keep doing this. There has to be a way to expose them."

Rehan hesitated. "It's not that simple. They've spent years silencing anyone who dares to speak out. Most of the people who know the truth are either missing... or dead."

Alex shivered, his face pale. "So we're up against a ghost?"

"Not exactly," Rehan replied, his voice low. "We're up against an organization that hides in plain sight. *The*

Machina is like a spider's web, with connections in every major city, every level of society. They manipulate information, control public perception... even police forces aren't free from their influence."

Ava felt a wave of frustration. "There has to be a weak spot, a way to reach them."

Rehan sighed, his gaze distant. "There might be one. There's a man—no one knows his real name, but people call him The Architect. He's rumored to be one of the original founders of *The Machina.* And if anyone has answers, it's him."

"Where can we find him?" Ava asked, a spark of hope igniting in her chest.

Rehan's expression darkened. "Finding him is the easy part. He's currently in Mumbai. The hard part is getting close. He's under constant protection, and rumor has it that he's paranoid. He moves locations frequently, never trusting anyone fully."

The silence that followed was tense. The idea of confronting the mastermind behind *The Machina* was both thrilling and terrifying.

As they discussed their next steps, Alex suddenly spoke, his voice unusually quiet. "I know where he'll be."

Ava and Rehan looked at him in surprise. "What do you mean?" Rehan asked, frowning.

Alex took a deep breath, his gaze fixed on the floor. "Before I joined *The Machina*, I used to run errands for someone high up in the organization—a recruiter who dealt with new initiates. He mentioned The Architect once, said he only appears for important events, like induction ceremonies."

Ava's eyes widened. "So if we find one of these ceremonies, we might find The Architect?"

Alex nodded, though his expression remained troubled. "Yes, but there's a catch. The ceremonies are heavily guarded, and only members of *The Machina* are allowed in."

Rehan narrowed his eyes, his mind working quickly. "Then we need a way to get you both in there. I'll stay outside to make sure we have a way out. But this... it's dangerous. One wrong move, and you'll be on their radar for good."

Ava met his gaze, her determination unwavering. "We have no choice. If we're going to stop them, we need to find The Architect. And if that means going into the lion's den, then that's what we'll do."

Rehan sighed, his face filled with concern, but he nodded. "Then let's get ready."

EIGHT

INTO THE DEN

Two nights later, Ava and Alex stood on a dimly lit street in an upscale neighborhood in Mumbai. The buildings around them were silent, looming like giants against the starlit sky. Rehan had chosen this location carefully, scouting it for any signs of *The Machina's* watchful eyes. He lingered a few blocks away, ready to step in if things went sideways.

Alex shifted uncomfortably in his disguise—a black suit and tie. He looked every bit the part of an elite recruit, his normally soft features hardened with a forced confidence. Ava, meanwhile, wore a sleek dress, her hair pulled back tightly, giving her a refined yet unapproachable appearance. They both bore expressions that masked their fear.

"Remember, stay calm and act like you belong," Rehan had warned them before they left. "They'll be watching for anyone who looks out of place."

As they approached the towering glass doors of the building, two security guards stood by, scrutinizing each guest as they entered. Ava's heart pounded, her pulse quickening as they drew closer. She forced herself to keep her head held high, her face impassive.

When it was their turn, Alex handed the guard a forged invitation, hoping that Rehan's contact had done their job well. The guard examined it, then gave them a curt nod, stepping aside to let them through.

The moment they entered the opulent lobby, Ava's senses went on high alert. The space was draped in sleek, modern decor, with soft lighting casting a cold glow over everything. It was a stark contrast to the chaos and noise of the Mumbai streets outside. People moved around them in quiet clusters, all dressed in the same polished attire, their expressions as guarded as their own.

Alex leaned toward Ava, his voice barely above a whisper. "We're in. Now what?"

She scanned the room, taking in every detail. "We need to find The Architect's quarters or his guards. If he's here, they won't be far."

A sudden murmur spread through the crowd as a man entered the room—a tall figure with an air of authority. His presence silenced the room, commanding immediate respect. He wore a crisp suit, and his face was shadowed, but Ava could feel the weight of his gaze. It was as if he saw straight through each person in the room.

"That's him," Alex whispered, his voice trembling slightly. "The Architect."

Ava's stomach twisted. The Architect's aura was chilling—cold and calculating. She felt an inexplicable fear, as though he could sense her motives, even from across the room. She fought the urge to look away, instead holding her posture steady.

But then, something unexpected happened. The Architect's gaze paused on them, his eyes narrowing ever so slightly. Ava felt her heartbeat spike, her mind racing. Had he recognized them? Or was it just paranoia seeping in?

The Architect motioned to one of his guards, who began moving in their direction. Ava's heart pounded, her mind scrambling for a plan. She whispered to Alex, "Act natural. Follow my lead."

The guard approached them, his expression unreadable. "Mr. Nair would like a word with you both."

They exchanged a quick, silent glance, then nodded, following the guard through the crowded room. The murmurs of conversation faded as they passed through a door at the back, entering a dimly lit hallway that led to a smaller, private room. Inside, The Architect waited, his back to them as he gazed out a window overlooking the city skyline.

When he finally turned to face them, his expression was unreadable, his eyes sharp and assessing. "I've been told that we have some new faces among us," he began, his voice smooth but with a hint of suspicion. "It's unusual for fresh recruits to attend an induction of this nature. Who do I have the pleasure of addressing?"

Ava steadied herself, meeting his gaze with as much confidence as she could muster. "My name is Ava. This is Alex. We're here because we believe in what *The Machina* stands for."

The Architect's eyes flickered, a small, unreadable smile tugging at his lips. "Is that so? And what is it, exactly, that you think we stand for?"

Ava hesitated, choosing her words carefully. "Power. Control. The ability to shape the world as we see fit, without the constraints society tries to impose on us."

The Architect's smile widened, though it didn't reach his eyes. "An intriguing answer. And you, Alex?" he asked, shifting his gaze to Alex.

Alex's voice trembled slightly as he spoke, but he managed to keep it steady. "We've both seen what the world is like... how it crushes people. We're ready to be part of something stronger."

For a moment, The Architect simply observed them, his gaze penetrating. Ava felt as if he were peeling back every layer of her thoughts, searching for any hint of deceit. Finally, he nodded.

"Ambition is a powerful motivator," he said, his tone approving. "But you must understand—joining *The Machina* requires more than just words. It demands loyalty... and sacrifice."

Ava swallowed, sensing the gravity of his words. She and Alex exchanged a quick glance, both knowing that this was the point of no return. If they wanted answers, they'd have to play this game carefully.

The Architect gestured to the door, his voice cold. "If you truly wish to prove yourselves, you will have an opportunity soon enough. Tonight is only the beginning. Until then... enjoy the evening."

They took the dismissal as an order, bowing slightly before turning to leave. As they stepped back into the crowded hall, Ava's mind reeled. She could feel the weight of The Architect's gaze on them, a silent warning that they were under scrutiny.

Rehan met them near the exit, his face tense. "Did he suspect anything?"

Ava exhaled, her pulse still racing. "I don't think he trusts us, but he didn't seem suspicious enough to stop us."

Alex nodded, though his hands were visibly trembling. "He's testing us, and he's going to watch our every move. This won't be easy."

Rehan's expression grew serious. "It won't, but you did well to get this close. Now, we need to use that trust to gather information about his next moves. We're in deep, but we're one step closer to knowing what *The Machina* is truly planning."

NINE

WHISPERS IN THE DARK

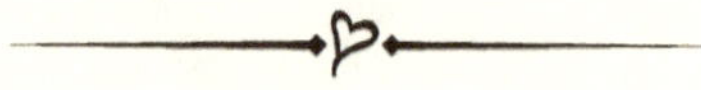

The following night, Ava and Alex returned to the towering building under the guise of dedicated recruits, blending into the sea of calculating faces. Their performance at the induction had clearly gained them some level of acceptance, but they knew better than to let their guard down. Rehan had warned them that *The Machina* monitored its members ruthlessly, testing loyalty through constant surveillance and manipulation.

Tonight, their task was simple: survive undetected and collect as much intel as possible.

Alex led Ava through the winding halls, their quiet steps echoing against the stark white walls. Security was heavy, with guards stationed at every corner. The buzz of low voices filled the air as other recruits murmured among themselves, but a sense of unease loomed over the room. It was as though everyone present was acutely aware that a single misstep could mean their end.

Ava kept her face composed, her gaze steady, yet her mind raced with questions. "We need to find a way to access

The Architect's private quarters or his documents," she whispered to Alex as they walked, making sure no one else could hear. "He might have files, plans, something that'll tell us what we're up against."

Alex nodded, his voice equally low. "Rehan mentioned there's a restricted section on the third floor. Only high-ranking members are allowed, but maybe we can find a way around that."

As they reached the elevator, Ava pressed the button for the third floor, her heart pounding. If they were caught, it would be over. But the doors slid open without any alarm, and they stepped in, feeling as if they were balancing on a knife's edge.

The third floor was eerily quiet, lit only by dim, bluish lights. The air felt colder here, more sterile, and Ava sensed that they were entering the true heart of *The Machina's* operations. As they walked down the hall, they passed several closed doors, each one marked with strange symbols rather than room numbers.

Suddenly, a shadow moved at the end of the hall. Ava froze, pulling Alex back into a nearby alcove. A guard walked past, oblivious to their presence, and disappeared around the corner. They exhaled in unison, then continued forward, even more cautious than before.

At last, they reached a large, steel door at the end of the corridor, marked only with a single, crimson emblem. Alex glanced at Ava, his expression grim. "This has to be it."

Ava nodded, steeling herself. She carefully examined the door and found a small keypad beside it. Pulling out the tiny hacking device Rehan had given them, she attached it to the keypad and watched as it worked, deciphering the code. After what felt like an eternity, the lock clicked open, and they slipped inside.

The room was dark, lined with shelves filled with binders, files, and maps. A single desk sat in the center, its surface cluttered with papers. Ava scanned the documents quickly, her eyes darting from one sheet to the next. Each page seemed to tell part of a larger story—a web of contacts, locations, and shipments that connected *The Machina* to powerful figures and shadowy organizations.

Alex whispered, "Look at this." He held up a file labeled *Project Genesis.*

Ava's stomach churned as she opened it. Inside, they found blueprints for a large facility, accompanied by notes detailing genetic experiments, human enhancement trials, and a chilling agenda: "To create a loyal and controllable human prototype. One that can serve without question."

"This... this is monstrous," Ava murmured, horrified. "They're experimenting on people, trying to turn them into... into machines."

Alex's face paled as he flipped through the pages. "They've been abducting people for these tests. It's why so many have disappeared without a trace."

Ava felt a surge of anger. *The Machina* wasn't just controlling minds—it was creating human weapons. She looked around the room, her resolve hardening. They had to get this information out, expose *The Machina* for what it truly was.

Just then, footsteps echoed from outside the door. Ava's heart stopped. Someone was coming.

"Quick, hide!" Alex whispered urgently, pulling her behind one of the shelves just as the door swung open.

A man entered, his face obscured in the shadows, but his voice unmistakable. It was The Architect. He moved to the desk, shuffling through some papers, and Ava could feel her pulse racing. They were trapped, barely a few feet away from the very man they sought to expose.

The Architect began speaking, as if addressing someone on the other side of a hidden earpiece. "Yes, the first phase of Project Genesis is nearly complete. Soon, we'll have the prototype. After that, nothing will stand in our way."

His words sent a chill down Ava's spine. She couldn't see his face, but the cold, calculated tone of his voice told her everything she needed to know. *The Machina* was planning something on a massive scale, and if they didn't act fast, countless lives would be destroyed.

The Architect finished his conversation, gathered a few files, and left the room. The moment the door closed, Ava and Alex slipped out from behind the shelf, their breaths shallow.

"We have to go," Ava whispered, clutching the *Project Genesis* file. "Rehan needs to see this. The world needs to see this."

They exited the room as quietly as they'd entered, their movements swift and silent. Every step felt like a race against time, and Ava's mind swirled with thoughts of what they'd uncovered. *The Machina* wasn't just manipulating people—it was creating weapons out of them, molding human lives into tools for their twisted vision.

As they made their way back to Rehan, Ava knew there was no turning back. They had declared war on *The Machina*, and the stakes were higher than ever. If they succeeded, they could bring the entire operation crashing down. But if they failed... they would become nothing more than another chapter in *The Machina's* dark history.

TEN

THE RECKONING

The air in Rehan's hideout was thick with tension as Ava and Alex poured over the information they had gathered from *The Machina*. The dim lighting cast long shadows on the walls, the flickering of a lone candle illuminating their anxious faces. A large map of Mumbai lay sprawled across the table, dotted with pins and notes, marking locations tied to *The Machina's* operations.

"Alright," Rehan began, his voice steady but low. "We have to act fast. *Project Genesis* is progressing quicker than I anticipated. We need to expose The Architect before he unleashes whatever he has planned."

Ava nodded, her resolve hardening. "But how? We can't just walk in there. The place is crawling with security."

Alex rubbed the back of his neck, his brow furrowed in thought. "What if we create a diversion? Something to pull their attention away while we slip in and gather what we need?"

Rehan's eyes gleamed with a hint of approval. "That could work. If we can disrupt their operations, it might buy us enough time to get inside. We need to gather allies too—people who can help us once we're in."

"But who can we trust?" Ava asked, glancing between the two of them. "We can't risk anyone tipping them off."

Rehan considered this for a moment before nodding. "There's a small group of defectors from *The Machina*—people who have seen the truth and escaped. If we can convince them to join our cause, we might stand a chance."

Alex took a deep breath, determination radiating from him. "Let's find them. We have to act now before it's too late."

With a plan in place, they set out into the night, their hearts pounding with the weight of what lay ahead. Rehan led them through the winding streets of Mumbai, avoiding the well-trodden paths and staying in the shadows, cautious of any lurking eyes.

Eventually, they arrived at a small, nondescript building on the outskirts of the city—a place Rehan claimed was a safe house for the defectors. As they approached the entrance, Ava felt a mix of hope and fear bubbling in her chest. This was their chance to gather the strength they needed, but what if these people were unwilling to help?

Rehan knocked three times on the weathered door, the sound echoing ominously in the stillness of the night. Moments later, a cautious face appeared in the crack of the door, eyes narrowing suspiciously at the trio.

"Rehan?" the voice questioned, laced with skepticism.

"It's me. I need to speak with the others—urgent business," he replied, glancing back at Ava and Alex for reassurance.

The door opened a fraction wider, and a woman stepped out, her face lined with weariness but her gaze sharp and assessing. "What have you brought us this time?"

As they entered the dimly lit interior, Ava took in the small group huddled together—ex-defectors from *The Machina*. They looked tired and worn, their expressions reflecting a mixture of hope and despair.

Rehan wasted no time, launching into their plan. "We've uncovered *Project Genesis*, and it's worse than we imagined. We need your help to stop it."

Murmurs spread through the group as they processed his words. Ava stepped forward, her heart pounding in her chest. "We're in a race against time. The Architect is building something that will change everything. We can't let him succeed."

A tall man with a rugged appearance stepped forward, his brow furrowed. "And why should we trust you? We've seen what *The Machina* does to traitors."

"Because I'm one of you," Ava said, her voice steady despite the tremor in her heart. "I've lost everything because of them. I want to see this end as much as you do."

Silence hung in the air, the weight of her words hanging heavily among them. After a moment, the woman who had greeted them spoke again. "If we join you, it'll be dangerous. We'll be risking our lives."

Alex stepped in, his voice urgent. "We understand that. But together, we have a chance to fight back. To make a stand against a force that has been preying on us for too long."

Slowly, one by one, the ex-defectors nodded, determination creeping into their expressions. They gathered around Ava and Alex, forming a small circle of resolve. It was a fragile alliance, but it was enough.

"Alright," the woman said, her voice steady. "We'll help you. But we need a solid plan if we're going to pull this off."

With their numbers bolstered, the group spent hours strategizing, pouring over maps and notes, plotting their approach. They discussed the layout of *The Machina's* headquarters, the timings of patrols, and potential escape routes.

As dawn broke, they finalized their plan. The group would split into two teams—one to create a diversion at the main entrance while the others slipped in through a service entrance. Ava, Alex, and Rehan would lead the second team, heading straight for The Architect's office.

As they prepared to leave, Ava felt a surge of adrenaline mixed with anxiety. "We can do this," she told the group, her voice ringing with newfound confidence. "We've come too far to turn back now."

With their hearts set on the path ahead, they moved as one, united in their mission to take down *The Machina* once and for all.

ELEVEN

THE CONFRONTATION

The sun hung low in the sky as the group prepared for the assault on *The Machina's* headquarters. A tension-filled silence wrapped around them, broken only by the sound of muffled footsteps and whispered commands. Ava's heart raced with anticipation and fear; they were on the brink of something monumental, and failure was not an option.

"Remember," Rehan said, his voice low but firm as they gathered in their makeshift command center. "Stick to the plan. We create the diversion, and then we get in, no matter what. We're counting on each other."

Ava nodded, determination burning in her chest. She could feel the weight of the moment pressing down on her. This wasn't just about her or Alex; it was about everyone who had suffered under *The Machina's* grip.

They moved through the dimly lit streets, the cool evening air a stark contrast to the heat of their resolve. As they approached the headquarters, Ava spotted the towering building looming before them, its windows glinting like dark eyes watching their every move.

In the distance, the first team was already in position, ready to create a distraction. They would set off fireworks near the main entrance, drawing guards and attention away from the service entrance where Ava, Alex, Rehan, and the others would slip in unnoticed.

"Here we go," Alex whispered, his hand brushing against Ava's shoulder. She looked at him, finding strength in his presence. They had come too far to turn back now.

With a nod from Rehan, the team moved into place. Suddenly, a loud explosion lit up the night sky, followed by the crackle of fireworks bursting into vibrant colors. The night lit up in chaos as shouts erupted from the guards, their attention drawn to the spectacle.

"Now!" Rehan commanded, and they raced toward the service entrance, slipping through the door before it could close.

Inside, the atmosphere was tense, the silence broken only by the distant sounds of alarm bells ringing. They quickly navigated the sterile hallways, guided by the map they had studied. Ava felt a mix of fear and exhilaration; they were close to their goal.

As they approached The Architect's office, Ava's pulse quickened. This was the moment they had worked so hard for, and she couldn't let fear paralyze her now. They reached the door, and Rehan signaled for silence.

"Alex, you and Ava stand watch. I'll breach the door," Rehan instructed. With a swift motion, he picked the lock, and the door swung open, revealing a dimly lit office filled with monitors and papers scattered across the desk.

"Stay alert," Alex whispered, positioning himself by the door as Ava stepped inside, her heart pounding. She scanned the room, taking in the sight of *The Machina's* secrets laid bare.

"Look at this," she breathed, moving to a nearby screen that displayed various surveillance feeds. Images of the streets, of people going about their lives, flashed before her. "They've been watching everyone."

Suddenly, a noise echoed from the hallway. Alex's eyes widened. "We need to hurry!"

They scrambled to search the desk, flipping through files and documents. Ava grabbed a folder titled *The Architect's Agenda*, her fingers trembling with urgency. Just then, the door burst open, and a squad of guards stormed in.

"Get down!" Alex shouted, pushing Ava to the floor as gunfire erupted around them. Ava felt a surge of adrenaline as she ducked behind the desk, her heart racing.

"Rehan!" she cried, desperately trying to find cover. The room erupted into chaos as the guards moved in, weapons drawn.

"Stay low!" Rehan shouted, returning fire as the room was filled with the sound of gunfire. Ava's mind raced; they had to get out and expose *The Machina*.

"Grab the files!" Alex yelled, still crouched behind the desk. "We need to take this information with us!"

Ava quickly stuffed the folder into her bag, her hands shaking. The guards were advancing, and they needed an exit strategy. "We can't fight them all! We need to find another way out!"

"Follow me!" Rehan shouted, leading the way to a side door at the back of the office. They burst through, emerging into a narrow hallway lined with darkened windows.

"We'll have to find another way down," Alex urged, glancing back at the approaching guards. "They're right behind us!"

As they ran, Ava's mind raced with possibilities. They had the information, but they needed to escape before *The*

Machina could close in on them. They reached a staircase leading down, and Rehan motioned for them to follow.

"Stay quiet and keep moving!" he urged, taking the lead. They descended quickly, adrenaline pushing them onward.

But just as they reached the bottom, they found themselves in a dimly lit corridor that opened into a large atrium. It was vast, filled with towering pillars and echoing with the sound of distant alarms.

"Where now?" Ava gasped, glancing around.

Before anyone could respond, The Architect stepped into view, flanked by several guards. His face was cold and unyielding, a sinister smile playing on his lips. "You think you can escape so easily?"

"Step aside!" Rehan demanded, raising his weapon. "We have what we came for!"

The Architect laughed, a chilling sound that reverberated off the walls. "You have no idea what you're up against. You think you can stop us? We are everywhere, and we control everything."

Ava felt a rush of fear but forced herself to remain calm. "This ends now," she declared, standing tall despite the overwhelming odds. "You can't keep controlling people's lives."

The Architect's smile faded slightly. "Oh, but I can. And I will. You've already lost."

With that, he raised his hand, signaling the guards to advance. Ava's heart raced, but she felt the weight of the files in her bag. They couldn't let this be the end.

"Together!" she shouted, rallying her friends as the guards closed in. They prepared to fight, determined to protect what they had uncovered and take down *The Machina* once and for all.

As the confrontation escalated, Ava realized that this was it—the climax of their battle against the shadows that had loomed over their lives. They were fighting not just for themselves but for everyone whose life had been stolen by *The Machina*. With courage surging through her veins, Ava braced herself for the fight of their lives.

TWELVE

THE FINAL STAND

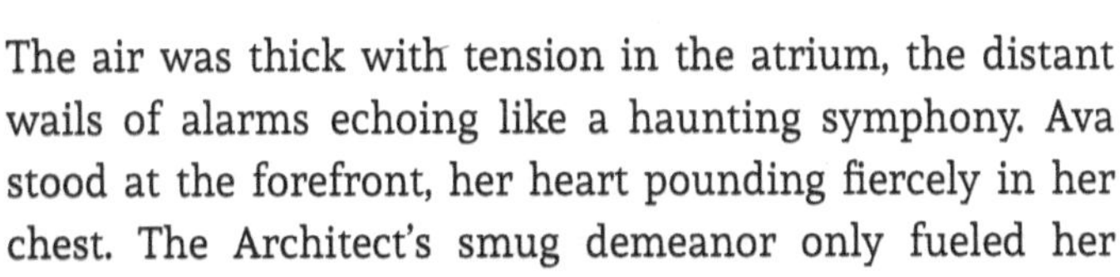

The air was thick with tension in the atrium, the distant wails of alarms echoing like a haunting symphony. Ava stood at the forefront, her heart pounding fiercely in her chest. The Architect's smug demeanor only fueled her determination. This was the moment they had prepared for, and she wasn't about to back down.

"Ready yourselves!" Rehan shouted, positioning himself defensively in front of Ava and Alex. The guards advanced, weapons raised, and the group braced for the inevitable clash.

"Do you really think you can win?" The Architect taunted, a cold glint in his eyes. "You're just children playing at being heroes. I control the future, and you're just a glitch in my plan."

Ava felt a rush of anger surge through her. "We're not glitches! We're the reckoning! You can't control people's lives anymore!"

As the first guard lunged forward, Rehan fired his weapon, hitting the man squarely in the shoulder. He went down, and chaos erupted. Guards poured into the atrium, and the air was filled with the deafening sounds of gunfire and shouted commands.

"Follow my lead!" Rehan shouted, moving quickly to create a barricade behind some nearby pillars. Ava and Alex fell in line, dodging bullets as they sought cover.

"We need to split up!" Ava shouted over the chaos. "If we can distract them, we might be able to reach The Architect!"

Alex nodded, determination etched on his face. "Let's do it! We can't let him escape!"

As they moved to execute their plan, Ava's mind raced. She had to think quickly. She spotted an emergency exit sign flickering in the distance. If they could draw the guards away, they might have a chance to corner The Architect.

"On my count," Rehan said, steadying his breath. "One... two... three!"

With a collective shout, they broke away from their cover, running in different directions. Ava sprinted toward the exit, adrenaline fueling her every step. Behind her, she could hear the shouts of guards as they scrambled to adjust, their attention divided.

Suddenly, a loud crash resonated from the opposite end of the atrium. Alex had knocked over a stack of crates, creating a barrier and drawing even more attention away from Ava and Rehan.

"Go, go, go!" Ava shouted, not looking back. They were almost there.

But just as they reached the emergency exit, The Architect stepped in front of them, a menacing figure framed by the dim light. "You think you can run?" he sneered. "You're not getting away that easily."

"Get out of our way!" Rehan shouted, aiming his weapon directly at The Architect. "This is your last chance."

The Architect laughed, a chilling sound that sent shivers down Ava's spine. "You have no idea what you're facing. I will rebuild this world, and you will be forgotten."

With a quick motion, he pulled out a sleek device from his pocket, pointing it at them. "Once I activate this, you won't just be forgotten; you'll be erased."

Ava's heart raced. "What does that do?" she demanded, stepping forward defiantly. "You're just a coward hiding behind your tech!"

"Enough!" The Architect roared, pressing the button. A low hum filled the air, and Ava felt a surge of energy ripple around them. "You'll see the consequences of defiance!"

In a moment of desperation, Ava lunged forward, tackling The Architect as the device began to glow ominously. The two of them crashed to the ground, struggling for control of the device.

"Stop!" Alex yelled, rushing to help Rehan subdue the guards. They were outnumbered, but they couldn't let The Architect win.

Ava felt a surge of strength as she fought to wrestle the device from The Architect's grasp. "We're not letting you destroy everything!" she cried, pushing against him with all her might.

With one final, desperate effort, Ava managed to wrench the device away from The Architect. She scrambled to her feet, holding it high. "This ends now!"

The Architect's expression shifted from smug confidence to shock as Ava pointed the device at him. "You don't have the guts to use it!" he sneered, but his bravado faltered as she activated it.

In an instant, the device whirred to life, and a brilliant light enveloped the room. The guards froze, confusion spreading among them. Ava felt the energy pulse through her, a wave of hope crashing over her.

"You'll regret this!" The Architect shouted, backing away as the light intensified.

"Not anymore," Ava declared, her voice steady as she directed the energy toward The Architect. With a flash, the light engulfed him, and he let out a scream of fury and despair.

As the light began to fade, Ava felt the weight of the device in her hand. The Architect was gone, erased from their reality. The remaining guards, seeing their leader defeated, hesitated and then dropped their weapons, fear replacing their aggression.

Ava, Alex, and Rehan exchanged astonished glances. "Did we really do it?" Alex breathed, disbelief etched on his face.

"Yes," Ava said, her voice trembling with emotion. "It's over."

In the aftermath, they gathered together with the ex-defectors, the atmosphere shifting from tension to relief. They had done the impossible—they had taken down *The Machina* and exposed The Architect's tyranny.

As dawn broke over Mumbai, casting a warm golden glow through the atrium windows, Ava felt a renewed sense of hope. They had fought for their freedom, and now they would help others reclaim theirs.

"Let's get out of here," Rehan said, a smile breaking through his weariness. "We have a lot of work ahead of us."

As they made their way out, Ava glanced back at the building that had held so much pain. It would take time to heal, but with their victory, they could begin to rebuild. Together, they would create a future free from the shadows of *The Machina*.

And as they stepped out into the light of a new day, Ava felt the weight of the world lift from her shoulders. She had found her strength, her purpose, and, most importantly, her family.

Together, they would change the world.

www.ingramcontent.com/pod-product-compliance
Lightning Source LLC
Chambersburg PA
CBHW021137130726
47988CB00003B/1351